THE MOUNTAIN BLUEBIRD

As this book was being completed, nearly one-half of Yellowstone National Park was burning. The sad news is that much living space has been changed by the sweeping forest and sageland fires. Time will tell how the fires of 1988 affect wildlife, but early reports are promising. Naturalists reported seeing bluebirds flock soon after the blazes died down. Large numbers of woodpeckers were also seen, apparently attracted by insects that suddenly appear after fires. And, I am happy to say, you will be able to visit the small grove of aspens near Slough Creek Campground. These beautiful trees and many other bluebird nesting forests were spared by the fires; the bluebirds will return to nest again.

Ron Hirschi,
Yellowstone National Park,
October, 1988

THE
MOUNTAIN BLUEBIRD

By RON HIRSCHI

Color photographs by GALEN BURRELL

Cobblehill Books/Dutton · New York

For Kevin and Lauren and their bright futures!

Acknowledgments

I am grateful to many people who helped directly and indirectly to make this book, especially all the encouraging supporters of OUR WILDLIFE. A deep thank you goes out to the members of the NORTH AMERICAN BLUEBIRD SOCIETY and to everyone along the Bluebird Trail. And, to Elsbeth—thanks for your story; to Rick—thanks for the gossamer kite tale; and to Rico—thanks for introducing me to the blue bird of happiness, of hope!

Library of Congress Cataloging-in-Publication Data

Hirschi, Ron.
   The mountain bluebird / Ron Hirschi; color photographs by Galen Burrell.
       p.   cm.
   Includes index.
   Summary: Text and photographs look at the life of that resident of the high valleys of the Rocky Mountains, the mountain bluebird.
   ISBN 0-525-65010-5
   1. Mountain bluebird—Juvenile literature. [1. Mountain bluebird. 2. Bluebirds.] I. Burrell, Galen, ill. II. Title.
QL696.P288H57   1989
598.8′42—dc19   88-32663
                                                          CIP
                                                          AC

Published in the United States by E. P. Dutton, New York, N.Y., a division of Penguin Books USA Inc. Published simultaneously in Canada by Fitzhenry & Whiteside Limited, Toronto

Designer: Charlotte Staub
Printed in Hong Kong
First edition   10 9 8 7 6 5 4 3 2 1

CONTENTS

A flock of mountain bluebirds on the snow in early spring around a yucca plant

INTRODUCTION

Even if you are never fortunate enough to see a flock of mountain bluebirds, you can create many images of them in your mind. Just by saying their name slowly to yourself, you might walk into their world of freshly fallen snow, paintbrush meadows, and mountain streams with bubbling, golden riffles. Mountains are inspiring places, blue a wonderful color.

The color blue is a symbol of hope and happiness in many cultures of the world. It paints the summer sky, the oceans, and the feathers of all three kinds of bluebirds that live in North

America. These birds wear the symbolic nature of their color well. Each began to disappear in recent decades, but populations have recovered in many places, all thanks to people who saw hope for the future of bluebirds and other wildlife.

Eastern bluebirds live on the Atlantic side of the Rocky Mountains. Western bluebirds range from the mountains to the Pacific. Both are similar to mountain bluebirds in many ways. All are members of the thrush family, a group of songbirds that includes the robin. Each feeds mainly on insects but will turn to berries as winter food. They all require a mix of woodland and meadow, spend much time on or near the ground, and require a cavity nest. This latter need is met by the bluebird houses put up for them when people noticed bluebirds vanishing from their skies.

You might see western, eastern, or mountain bluebirds along the miles of bluebird trails that link individual birdhouses together in pathways throughout North America. The birds and their new houses perch atop fenceposts in backyards, along farmer's fields, and at the edges of country roads as well as busy freeways.

Where their ranges overlap, you will have little trouble distinguishing a mountain bluebird from its relatives. Both eastern and western bluebirds wear a splash of red on their breasts, coloring that usually sneaks up a bit higher on the shoulders and back of a western. Mountain bluebirds lack this red feathering and males are truly blue birds. But, their main distinguishing feature is their mountain way of life.

They need the high valleys of the western mountains, mountains that divide the North American continent as sharply as they separate eastern from western bluebirds. I hope this book will introduce you to this beautiful area as much as it introduces you to the mountain bluebird. They are inseparable from one another—mountain and bird—and once we have a sense of the strength of their relationships, we will learn something far greater about what binds us all to these magnificent snowcapped peaks, bluebirds, and clean mountain streams.

Male eastern bluebird

Male western bluebird

Female western bluebird

The mountains where the bluebirds live

BLUEBIRD SPRING

Follow a flock of mountain bluebirds across the high plains border of the Rocky Mountains. Wind whistles through their wings as they fly in loose formation, just above the silver-green sage. Each bird rises and falls like a ripple in a wave, a wave that leads the slow advance of spring to the foot of the western mountains.

Looking for a place to rest, the bluebirds drop from the sky at the entrance to a river canyon. They settle to the ground, perching on freshly fallen snow. With feathers fluffed for added

8

warmth, the birds huddle close together. How could we ever know how cold they feel?

Soon, warmer weather will be on its way. Already, green blades of new plant growth poke through the thin layer of late season snow. On the hillsides above, the tips of aspen trees swell as tender leaves begin to uncurl from their winter buds.

Overhead, the sun's rays pierce thin puffs of cloud. Patches of blue show through. But, no blue, not even the brightest summer sky, seems as blue as the bluebirds of spring.

The brightest blue of these spectacular birds are males. Like the color of the sky, their feathering varies greatly. Some individuals are a deep cobalt blue. Turquoise is worn by others. Some males wear a soft pastel not yet captured in any box of paints.

Females have a subtle and surprising beauty all their own. While sitting near the brighter colored males, female mountain bluebirds might remain unnoticed. Their pale blue to gray-brown backs blend well with the dry grasses of the plains. But, their breast feathers seem to be sprinkled with freshly ground cinnamon. Their folded flight feathers are etched with a faint touch of blue. When they fly, the females' wings spread to reveal striking patterns, often a royal blue as beautiful as that worn by any male.

Yet, the beauty of bluebirds in spring contrasts sharply with the realities of their lives.

The mountains and high plains offer abrupt and extreme temperature changes, sudden snowstorms in any month, and biting winds that would freeze your fingertips. In West Yellowstone, Montana, for example, temperatures fell below freezing every night in April, 1986, and dipped to a low of −5°F. on the night of April 14th. That same year, temperatures were as low as 19°F. during the last week of May and dropped to 29°F. on the night of June 22nd, even though it was a very warm 80°F. the following afternoon.

Still, as early as March, these tiny birds (measuring about six inches from tip of bill to tip of tail, adult bluebirds weigh

Mountain bluebirds in early spring

Male mountain bluebird

Female mountain bluebird

9

A mountain bluebird nest hole in a dead aspen tree

approximately one ounce; it would take a dozen bluebirds to equal the weight of a can of soda) leave the plains, fly up river canyons, and attempt to find places to nest in mountain valleys. Their search is made all the more difficult because they nest in very special places that must have cavities with entry holes. The holes must be large enough for them to squeeze through, yet small enough to keep out predators, rain, and freezing snow.

Males often arrive first at these cavity nesting sites, claiming territories defended in ways that clearly show the high value of a chosen nesting place.

Intruding males are warned not to enter another's territory in several ways. A singing male uses his voice to announce his presence. He also makes his territorial boundaries known during flights around the nesting area. Like all birds, bluebirds depend a great deal on vision and have little difficulty advertising their presence since their bright plumage can be seen from considerable distances.

Willows begin to change color in early spring at about the same time that mountain bluebirds arrive.

If a rival male ignores all warnings, the defender responds with a flash of blue feathers. He first tries to chase the intruder away. If that fails, he will hover over his rival, flapping his wings as a warning signal.

In an uncommon show of fury, a male bluebird bursts into battle if intruders persist.

A defending male flies up to the intruder, striking feet first. Locking claws in midair, they tumble to the ground. Bouncing and rolling, they flap their wings, snapping at one another with their small, yet sharp beaks. Feathers fly.

Eventually, the combatants untangle. The battle may be repeated, but the outcome usually favors the defending male and neither bird appears to receive serious injury. It is also thought that such intense battles usually do not occur unless the male has been joined at the nest site by a female.

The sequence of events during the breeding season varies from place to place with nesting beginning earlier at low elevations and in more southerly latitudes. Springtime climbs mountains slowly and moves northward at about the same pace.

In some areas, females accompany males when the nest search first begins. This has led some people to assume that bluebirds mate for life, choosing partners sometime in early spring when winter flocks begin to break up into smaller groups of birds.

There is evidence to suggest that some bluebirds will mate with another partner in following years. But, it is likely that some do stay with a single mate throughout their lifetimes. During a single season, bluebirds are typically monogamous and, like many other aspects of their life history, closer study is needed to understand sexual relationships more clearly.

It may be more important for their survival to study their relationships with the mountains and valleys they need as spring and summer homes.

Long before a mountain valley can support a breeding pair of bluebirds, it must be shaped by forces far beyond the birds' control. These natural forces create ideal conditions for bluebird nesting sites and allow room for many other animals.

Male mountain bluebirds often arrive first at the nesting sites.

A mountain bluebird pair

Mountain bluebirds live only in the mountains and high plains of western North America, such as here on Mount Rainier, where they nest at treeline.

The natural shaping of mountain valleys began many thousands of years ago. It continues today, even though people have interfered in many ways. You can see mountains take on new shapes if you watch logging crews work, bulldozers cut new roadways, or dam builders flood river valleys. You can also watch natural changes. They are best seen each year when snow falls, thaws, then washes into mountain streams.

At first, falling snow seems as threatening to bluebirds as a bulldozer. It is cold, wet, and covers feeding places. But, snow is also the greatest reservoir of moisture, storing water in its frozen crystals until the sun melts the winter's covering. This clean water is precious to life.

Snow-fed streams are also one of the most important physical forces that continually shape and reshape mountains.

These streams are far more valuable than gold they often wash from mountainsides as they slowly carve each peak into ever smaller pieces. Over time, they cut into the mountains, beginning at the highest points where there is little room for life of any kind. Slowly, ever so slowly, they wash deeper into the rugged stone.

Just as slowly, mountain life begins to appear along the streambanks and valley sides.

The rugged shoulders of each mountain are eventually smoothed by stream erosion. Soil builds up in the valleys. Meadow plants sprout. Trees grow and forests climb the mountainsides. As plant growth becomes more abundant, birds and mammals flourish.

This sequence of events leading to the creation of mountain valleys that could support bluebirds takes place in all mountain ranges of the world. Yet, the special magic of life is complex. There are no mountain bluebirds in the Andes. None in the Swiss Alps. No bluebirds grace the high Himalayas. Not even the sacred Mount Fuji of Japan can claim their presence.

Mountain bluebirds only live in the mountains and high plains of western North America. Why is not clearly understood.

12

It is clear that the mountains of the American West are undergoing more rapid changes now than at any time in history. Our roads, logging, dam building, and other activities have severely altered the natural pace of change in the mountains.

Sometimes, the new changes happen so quickly that bluebirds and other animals cannot adapt. Most times, the changes are so complex that we do not see their results soon enough or clearly enough to understand what is happening to animals affected by our actions. That is why it is so important to study and to understand places where natural processes are dominant in shaping mountain valleys.

It is also exciting to see these places where mountain wildlife thrives and is ever-changing in ways not adversely affected by people. Fortunately, relatively unchanged river valleys remain. One you might visit is the upper Shell Creek Valley in the Bighorn Mountains that stretch across the northern border of Wyoming into Montana.

Shell Creek begins in snowfields that melt each spring to expose vast meadows that carpet the Bighorn high country. The stream originates almost 12,000 feet above sea level within the Cloud Peak Wilderness Area. It then winds through pine forest, plunges through spectacular canyons, and slips past rimrock eroded over hundreds of centuries. This is sacred land to many people. It is also a place you can easily visit, pitching your tent within sight of a mountain bluebird nest.

Mountain bluebirds return to Shell Creek each spring. They have come here since long before the first people passed this way in search of elk and deer, a route to the west, or Bighorn gold. But, the bluebirds are selective, not nesting in every part of Shell Creek canyon.

How will you begin a search to discover where they nest and learn what a bluebird family needs to survive?

You might begin early in the morning after fishing for trout or watching dippers dive for breakfast in the fast-flowing waters passing through Shell Creek Campground. The stream has beautiful golden riffles and is difficult to leave. Fishing is great.

Flyfisherman on the Yellowstone River during the summer salmonfly hatch. The large stoneflies provide food for many animals and sport for people who gather here from all over the world.

Dragonflies are also eaten by bluebirds. Like the stonefly, early life stages of the familiar dragonfly are spent beneath the water's surface. These nymphs crawl out of the water, then go through a metamorphosis as they become winged adults.

But, if you climb above Shell Creek, you will be able to trace its historical path as you walk up the mountainside that this stream helped to create. You will also see many animals it helps to sustain.

Climb through the meadow that rises abruptly, above the cottonwood and pine trees that shade the stream. With each step, swarms of insects fly into the air. Among them are delicate mayflies and clumsy-bodied stoneflies that crawl onto meadow grasses to dry their wings while completing their life cycle. Did you know they first sprang to life in the waters of Shell Creek? Before most of them are able to fly beyond this valley, they will be eaten by wrens, flickers, sapsuckers, warblers, flycatchers, lazuli buntings, baby blue grouse, and by mountain bluebirds.

Climb higher still to where boulders, old logs, and tangles of wild rose dot the meadow. While you catch your breath on a lichen-covered rock, imagine the centuries it took to create this valley, remembering that Shell Creek once flowed right at your feet. Remember too, that the lupine, rose, and wild geraniums blooming in the meadow were covered with snow not too many weeks before.

Listen to the wind whisper through the soft petals of the wild-flowers. Watch their seeds drift on the breeze before falling to moist places where they might take root. Watch, too, for thick clouds to roll over the crest of the nearby ridges, threatening a rain shower.

Jump from your resting place. Run up the hill. Take cover from the rain beneath the aspen trees perched on the gently sloped ledge overlooking the meadow.

While you wait for the rain to stop, a wren might fly up to your side, scolding you for intruding. A curious mule deer might peek through the tree trunks, searching for your hiding place. Stay quiet. The deer will walk past as you listen to the sounds of the mountains.

One of the gentlest sounds you will hear is a near whisper of a song that comes from a bird, likely sitting on the same rock where you rested moments before. There, in the middle of the lupine blossoms, a soft, *"Scheer, Scheer, Scheer,"* rises from a fluff of blue sitting next to a silent sparrow.

House wrens also nest in holes in trees in areas where mountain bluebirds nest.

Ron Hirschi

Aspen groves provide shelter for many animals, including mule deer, bears, chipmunks, elk, and moose.

15

A female mountain bluebird sits in an aspen tree and then flies down to her nest which is in a hole in a dead aspen tree.

The bluebird leaps up to snatch a mayfly, flutters to a branch just above your head, then pops into a round hole neatly chiseled into the clean, white bark of an aspen.

Crouch nearby, trying not to disturb the parent birds as they both come and go to care for their young. Look out as they fly from the nest to search for food. The bluebirds' aspen sits at the edge of the forest, at the edge of the meadow, and, it seems, at the very edge of the earth itself.

If you visit Alberta, the Colorado Rockies, the Oregon Cascades, or the Sangre de Cristo Range in New Mexico, try to find similar valleys. Thinking like a bluebird and listening like a deer, you will discover where nests should be.

If at first you don't hear the bird's soft song or see its blue wings hovering over the meadow, you will know where to look. You will also know how a bluebird's search begins when it leaves the high plains, separates from the winter flocks, and flies up a river canyon to find a place to raise its young. Its nest might be in a tree other than an aspen. But, it will often be along the forest edge, near the safety of a tangle of wild rose, within view of a mountain stream, and within sound of the constant buzz of insects flying above a meadow sprinkled with wildflowers.

This is a bluebird's spring and summer home.

16

The Shell Creek aspen forest

From Alaska to Arizona and New Mexico, you might discover mountain bluebirds nesting in aspen meadows similar to the grove perched above Shell Creek. Jasper and Banff in the Canadian Rockies, Yellowstone, Grand Teton National Park, and other of the least-spoiled western landscapes offer pristine bluebird nesting places. Bluebirds also nest on the slopes of Mt. St. Helens, recently devastated by a volcanic eruption and more recently recolonized by insects, mammals, and birds.

Wherever they search for a nest, bluebird pairs excitedly

EXCAVATORS, COMPETITORS, AND PREDATORS

17

A female mountain bluebird with an insect for young at her nest box

explore cavities in tamarack, spruce, pine, fir, aspen, and other trees. They will also nest in holes in cliffs, sandbanks, and in bridges. Like eastern and western bluebirds, they will move into nest boxes with little hesitation. At times, they even choose strange crevices within objects not necessarily meant for their use.

Once, a bluebird pair nested in the grill of a Chevy sedan parked in front of a house near West Yellowstone, Montana. The car's owner noticed the birds flying in and out of a gap just beneath the headlight and waited patiently for the female to sit on the eggs before driving the few miles into town. By the time they hatched, the nestlings had already covered many miles, probably more than any bluebirds alive. Soon, the car's owner needed to drive more often to her bookshop in town. Since the road was bumpy and the nestlings are delicate, she decided to move the nest.

She carefully removed the cup of grass that surrounds the baby birds, lifting it from the grill when the parents had flown off to feed. The nest was tucked inside a cinder block and set atop a stepladder not far from the car. Probably directed by their nestlings' hunger calls, the parents readily flew to the new location. As they would in a more remote location, the male and female continued to feed their offspring, raising them successfully.

The following year, no bluebirds returned to nest in the Chevy's grill or in the cinder block. But, bluebirds do return to nest again in the same places in more favorable locations. Sometimes.

No one knows how often they might reuse a nest or what conditions are needed for a bluebird pair to raise more than one family, together or with a new mate, in the same place. We do know one thing is far more important than any other to encourage bluebirds to nest even once, no matter what the location: the nest hole.

The natural processes leading to the creation of meadows, aspen groves, and abundant insects make little difference to bluebirds if holes cannot be found. Bluebirds are unable to excavate their own nest chambers.

Unfortunately, too many bluebirds return each year to devastated woodlands where their favorite old trees have vanished due to unmanaged logging, woodcutting, or clearing for increasing numbers of people.

Fortunately, people build nest boxes to replace some of these old trees and their natural cavities. The boxes provide an important nesting need. But birdhouses are somewhat like tents in the wilderness when compared with the natural homes they attempt to replace. Like tents, they may only offer temporary shelter lacking the support for long-term survival.

People put up nest boxes as an essential aid to birds facing a housing crisis. But the continued survival of bluebirds is linked to interrelationships and needs of many kinds of plants and animals. When nesting sites vanish, it is easy to replace an aspen grove with boxes. But we don't know if the nest houses will continue to be the best way to insure that bluebirds will return year after year.

It is probably more valuable to protect mountain meadows, aspen groves, and other wildlife that share and shape bluebird homes.

Throughout their long history, bluebirds have depended on aspens, streams, and many kinds of animals. We are just beginning to understand the simplest elements of their world, the most basic of their relationships. We are also just beginning to appreciate how some events, such as snowfall, can be harmful at times and beneficial at others.

Probably the most important and most colorful group of animals that play a major role in the lives of mountain bluebirds is the woodpeckers.

Woodpeckers can be thought of as the master architects, carpenters, and real estate salespeople of the bird world. They excavate uniquely designed homes for themselves, typically moving on to a new tree each year. They also drill holes while feeding, and create cavities to sleep in or to get in out of the

A female flicker

19

A yellow-bellied sapsucker on a dead aspen. It drills neat rows of tiny holes in fruit and other trees to tap the supply of sap from the trees. Its nest hole is just the right size for bluebirds.

weather. When woodpeckers abandon their old homes, bluebirds and others incapable of building their own nesting chambers will move in.

Walk through any forest in early spring. Listen for woodpecker tapping. That sound is often the sound of construction. Sometimes it is the sound of playful advertisement. Meant for the ears of other woodpeckers, the distinctive rapping and tapping will attract a mate or warn others to stay away. The sound may also attract bluebirds.

As you walk beneath the trees, watch for potato-chip-sized chunks of wood dropping from above. These identify the presence of a pileated woodpecker. This elegant, crow-sized bird with a flaming red topnotch excavates holes big enough to be used later by goldeneyes, squirrels, owls, and wood ducks.

The flicker, a slightly smaller woodpecker, creates neat, round holes about 2¾ inches in diameter. An entrance just right for later use by saw-whet owls, kestrels, and buffleheads, the flicker's home is apparently too large for bluebirds.

Mountain bluebirds need smaller holes drilled by other kinds of woodpeckers. Especially valuable are the 1½-inch or slightly larger holes chiseled by hairy woodpeckers, yellow-bellied sapsuckers, and Williamson's sapsuckers.

Competition for the woodpeckers' old homes can be intense. Hairy woodpeckers will try to reuse their same nesting places year after year. Swallows, chickadees, nuthatches, squirrels, and wrens search for the vacancies. A healthy forest must have lots

Ground squirrels live in meadows near bluebird nests.

of holes to make sure there will be enough homes for everyone.

A dramatic example of a filled-to-capacity forest can be seen in a small aspen grove just above Slough Creek Campground in the northeast corner of Yellowstone Park.

You might camp here, then walk through a July morning, listening for baby birds begging breakfast while your parents cook pancakes or fry hashbrowns and eggs. Follow the bird sounds, turning off the horse trail that winds its way to upper Slough Creek Meadows, McBride Lake, and Buffalo Plateau. The aspen grove sits between the pine-forested trail and a boulder-strewn knoll where moose like to nap.

Be careful not to disturb the moose as you walk through this small patch of aspens. Several of the trees are broken topped. Some are completely dead but still standing; known as snags, each of these old trees seems to sing.

Paintbrush and tall grass fill the spaces between each tree trunk. Open mouths of baby sapsuckers, flickers, chickadees, nuthatches, and mountain bluebirds fill the entry spaces of the many nest holes in this tiny forest. While the baby birds chirp, chipmunks and red squirrels pop in and out of the few cavities unoccupied by birds.

The Slough Creek aspen grove is teeming with life because old trees, including dead snags, are protected within the National Park. Similar protection is lacking in most forests even though snag protection is being slowly extended, with difficult opposition, to other places.

Recent studies suggest that forests should contain about six snags per acre to make sure cavity-nesting animals have enough room to breed. But, these guidelines are too general to fit many locations. As the Slough Creek aspens demonstrate, at least seven different cavity-nesting birds and mammals will live in a forest of only twenty trees. All this new life is in a space no larger than a small backyard or an elementary school classroom.

Grandparents of the forest, old trees offer shelter needed by many baby animals tucked within their nests. Like human grandchildren, bluebirds and their nesting competitors will

Western tanagers live in the same areas as mountain bluebirds.

Paintbrush near summit of Mount Washburn

21

Bluebird predators include prairie falcons. This baby falcon just ate a bird and is waiting for the return of its parent.

fight, as if for a grandparent's attention, when the old trees are in short supply.

Remove all the old trees and chaos results.

First, the woodpeckers vanish because there are fewer trees on which to search for food and no old trees in which to drill nest holes. Without woodpeckers, where will chickadees, nuthatches, squirrels, and bluebirds find homes to move into?

Loss of nesting trees and decreasing woodpecker populations may be the greatest threats to bluebirds. This is evident in places where nest boxes are put up and populations increase.

Severe competition from starlings and house sparrows also displaces bluebirds. This threat is more common where human settlement attracts these exotic pests. It is also a more common threat to western and eastern bluebirds since they live at lower elevations where these competitors thrive.

Other threats include insecticides that eliminate bluebird food, land clearing that eliminates bluebird feeding places, severe winters, and abrupt changes in spring weather.

Individual bluebirds are snatched by predators including Cooper's hawks, sharp-shinned hawks, and merlins. Normally, these predators don't threaten bluebird populations, however, since a hawk's survival depends on its prey's survival.

Bluebird losses also occur during scientific studies. A recent research project involved the killing of one member of several bluebird pairs to see how mates would respond. Another allowed people to remove nestlings to artificially manipulate numbers being fed by parent birds. Should we allow scientists to kill bluebirds to learn what a bluebird mate might do or how much time parents spend feeding their young?

Or, should we begin watching living bluebirds more closely, attempting to learn how they survive despite predation, competition for nesting places, and loss of their woodland meadows? In answering these questions, we might learn a great deal more about bluebirds. We might also learn how to get along with others if we study the relationships between animals sharing the bluebirds' mountain valleys.

22

A mother dipper flies up to her fledgling in Shell Creek.

Pine scent drifts through the warm summer air as thick as the cloud of insects rising from the surface of the Yellowstone River. The pine odor fills every gap along the river, the sedge meadows near its banks, and the pale green sage prairies that lead into the surrounding forest. For the bluebirds nesting along this edge of sage and pine within Yellowstone Park, much more than the summer fragrance connects them with the river.

Look closely along the riverbank and you will see why so many nest holes face the stream.

SUMMER
TO FALL

23

From beneath stones in the middle of the river, a prehistoric-looking aquatic insect crawls out and onto the bank. It is a stonefly, leaving its river way of life to undergo a quick change during metamorphosis that turns its alligator-like body into a winged form.

Salmonflies are among the most abundant stoneflies. Each summer, thousands of them emerge at the same time. When they appear, they create a feeding frenzy in and alongside the river. The rapids are filled with hungry trout. Flycasters from all over the world gather to cast imitation salmonflies at rings that mark the spots where fish slurp their seemingly endless meals. River otters, harlequin ducks, raccoons, and adult bluebirds join the feast.

If the timing of the nesting season is just right, baby bluebirds will soon fly and join their parents during this peak of food abundance. But, nesting success in the mountains is unpredictable. Sometimes, it ends in failure.

Even though the calendar says summer, winter weather often descends with no warning, chilling the air inside bluebird nests. Snow sometimes falls just as the babies hatch. Icy winds often sweep away the clouds of insects rising from the river and from the mountain meadows.

Fishers of trout can head for warm shelters during these abrupt changes of weather. River otters can switch from a salmonfly diet to crayfish or squawfish. Harlequin ducks can dive beneath the rapids to eat salmonfly nymphs. Raccoons can eat almost anything. But, bluebirds must be able to find insects above the water's surface. If they can't catch enough, their nestlings will die.

Sadly, this is a common cause of bluebird mortality.

Probably as an adaptation to the severities of mountain life, bluebirds will nest a second, third, and possibly a fourth time. Even when they successfully raise a set of nestlings, a bluebird pair will begin again the nest building, feeding, and other duties of parenting.

Like their first nest site, the second cavity is searched for with

Ron Hirschi

Mountain bluebirds now nest in the wooden posts surrounding a stone marker at the grave of one of the first white women to live in Yellowstone National Park during winter.

much excitement. Holes are examined, defended, and finally chosen by a mated pair. Who does the final selection is not certain. The female seems to have all the responsibility for building the nest.

She picks up dry grasses as soon as the weather returns to a calmer pattern of warm days and a lack of snow. She spends almost a week carrying the nest material into the cavity, usually lining the cup-shaped nest with feathers. She then lays a single egg each day, waiting until her clutch is completed before beginning to incubate.

A first clutch often contains six eggs. Second sets are often limited to five or fewer. These pale blue eggs are carefully attended to by the female.

Mother bluebirds sit on the eggs while the male perches in a nearby tree. When leaving to feed, she is usually accompanied by her mate. But, they do not travel far, often confining these feeding flights to distances shorter than one hundred yards. They will also feed right beneath the nest.

Although the adults consume large insects, including the salmonflies, they switch to a search for tiny insects when their young hatch after about a two-week incubation. At first, the babies are nearly naked and weigh about four grams (about ⅛ the weight of their parents; it would take almost one hundred newborns to equal the weight of a can of soda).

Sparse down soon appears on the nestlings. But this thin layer offers little insulation and the first week of life outside the egg requires a mother's warmth. She broods her young during this critical period, sheltering them from the cold nights.

A male bluebird will feed its mate while she broods their young, but the female also leaves the nest during this time. As the nestlings grow stronger, both parents must spend considerable time catching insects for their hungry babies. They also remove fecal waste from the nest.

In the first weeks, this waste from the young is neatly packaged in a white pouch known as a fecal sac. The sacs are carried away by the parent birds on trips away from the nest.

A male mountain bluebird shares nesting duties after the young have hatched. He also stands guard while the female sits on the eggs.

The male flies from the nest carrying the fecal sac. Note: to avoid harmful disturbance, no photographs were taken of young inside the nesting cavities.

25

Gradually, the baby birds' down is replaced with feathers. Typically, the young are ready to leave the nest about three weeks after hatching. This can be as early as June for a first set of nestlings or as late as the end of July or early August for second nests.

Weak flyers at first, the fledglings are led to clumps of wild rose or other dense shrubs where they can hide from predators. Parents hover over their young, coaxing them to follow when all is safe.

After about two or three weeks, the young birds gain enough experience on the wing to fly to the tops of tall trees. From a distance, they appear to move through the air as gracefully as their parents. They also seem indistinguishable from the adults. Up close, their appearance and their behavior readily identify them as fledglings. Their backs are pale blue-gray like their mother, but the young birds' breasts are flecked with spots somewhat like a baby robin's. And, they continually flutter their wings to beg for food.

Watch them closely. You will see that newly fledged birds seem to notice very little going on around them. The meadow

A baby bluebird just out of the nest along the Firehole River in Yellowstone Park. Its spotted breast identifies it as a fledgling and shows a resemblance to young of relatives such as robins and thrushes.

Ron Hirschi

26

must be a blur in their eyes; all attention is focused on their parents.

For the first few weeks outside the nest, fledglings do not watch for fluttering moths, mayflies, or even the juicy body of the dual-winged salmonflies. Stimulated by the persistent wing flapping of their begging offspring, adults seem to have time for watching little else.

Adult bluebirds usually hunt on the ground, or from a low perch. But, they will drop from the tops of trees 75 feet or more above the ground to catch slow-moving salmonflies as they flutter above the riverbank. Bigger than most grasshoppers, with wingspans of about three inches, these stoneflies are more than a beakful, and bluebirds have a hard time holding on to them.

Dropping a still struggling salmonfly to the ground, a bluebird parent will hover, then pounce on its prey. Pressing the insect against a log or stone, the bird tears its catch into small pieces. These are fed to the young birds that eagerly follow mother and father bluebird on hunting trips.

Sometimes, baby bluebirds only have a father to follow since females will renest before the young birds are fully independent.

When independence arrives is not clear. Young bluebirds are able to hunt insects on their own about three weeks after leaving the nest, perhaps sooner. They may try to stay near their parents after this time and some fledglings have been observed to help feed their parent's next set of nestlings.

Other observations suggest that young bluebirds are driven away by their parents. As is the case with most animals, variations in these family interactions are to be expected. This is especially true for mountain bluebirds due to the unpredictable nature of mountain life.

Throughout the warm days of late summer, young bluebirds do gather in larger flocks. Adults often vanish from sight at this time, apparently seeking a safe place to molt the bright feathers they have worn since spring. They later rejoin flocks of young birds, possibly gathering with their own offspring.

These late summer and early fall flocks still feed along rivers.

Soon after the young birds leave the nest, adults molt, losing their brightest spring feathers. They are able to fly at this time, but they seem less active.

They also sweep through sage meadows and more open prairie, flying just above the ground, dropping suddenly to pounce on a moth, beetle, or ant.

The flocks may number only a few birds or as many as fifty or more. All of these groups seem to move from place to place quickly, not staying long in any one location. They may be accompanied by chipping sparrows, juncos, or yellow-rumped warblers at this time. But, mountain bluebirds do not appear to gather in mixed species flocks as readily as many other songbirds. They do feed in many of the same high meadows where elk herds gather, Canada geese graze, and coyotes and weasels hunt for mice.

As days grow shorter and nights cooler, the bluebirds seem restless. It is as if they anticipate the long migration soon to come. By day and by the light of the moon their restlessness heightens. After all, this is one of the most dramatic times in their year. Like Christmas. Or, like the nights before a championship soccer game, the bluebirds even begin to sleep less.

In German, the word *zugunruhe* defines most clearly this premigratory restlessness displayed by many birds about to journey south. Before they begin that migration, however, many mountain bluebirds take a brief journey that leads them in an unexpected direction.

This late summer movement does not lead south, or even to lower elevations. Instead, many bluebirds turn upriver, rise above timberline, and fly to the summits of the highest peaks within the surrounding mountain ranges.

You might see bluebirds at this time, tiny specks of blue brushing past alpine meadows near the summit of 10,000-foot-high Mount Washburn in Yellowstone Park. They settle in bare branches of the scattered trees growing at this elevation, then drop to the leeward side of the mountain. Rising and falling in their characteristic flight, some swoop past. Others hover on warm winds rising from the valleys below, then drop to the ground to snatch ants, beetles, and spiders crawling about on the paintbrush, cinquefoil, and mountain heather.

Ron Hirschi

Wild rose

28

Ron Hirschi

Bluebirds feed in many of the same high meadows where elk herds gather.

This high elevation gathering may last through September. As one flock flies from the mountain, another takes its place in continuous waves of ascending birds. In some mountain ranges, bluebirds fly up to even greater heights of 12,000 feet or more. What draws them to such heights above any nesting possibilities?

Even more plentiful than salmonflies in early summer, a wealth of spiders and ants, beetles and mayflies, moths and caddisflies, and other insects appear on the mountaintops each year. They arrive as if from nowhere. At the highest points, even on the eternal snowfields of glaciated peaks, bluebirds are suddenly able to pick an incredible abundance of food from the surface of the mountains.

Some of the bluebirds' late summer prey emerge from alpine meadows, late in blooming due to the slow arrival of "spring" at high elevations. Most, literally tons of them, are swept up the mountains by warm air currents that flow like windy rivers.

At lower elevations, insects are plucked from the air as these

Mountain bluebird in the alpine in early fall

Male mountain bluebird looking for insects

warm air currents drift up river valleys. Rising on the updrafts, the swarms of tiny hitchhikers float to the high peaks and beyond. Bluebirds probably take advantage of these same warm winds that offer an easy flight and an abundance of food at journey's end.

Several kinds of insects and most spiders seem willing participants in this high altitude migration. Flying ants march to high points, then fly up to catch a warm updraft that carries them to new surroundings. Wolf spiders crawl on delicate legs, climbing to the highest branches of trees and snags as if searching for perfect launching sites. Then, they reach up on their many toe tips, shoot out silk threads, and feel the rising air pull their strings. Letting go, they allow the air currents to drag them into the sky like kites on the breeze.

Flying on their gossamer strings, spiders drift with no control of their movements. Some soar over the mountains, drifting on air streams well above 20,000 feet. In another land, spiders have been found at the highest point on earth, atop Mount Everest.

It is not surprising then, that spiders appear atop high peaks in the Rockies, Cascades, and Sierras. It is also not surprising that bluebirds gather on these high slopes to feast at summer's end. Spiders, ants, and streamborn insects deposited on mountain peaks are some of the most abundant sources of food at this time of year. When they fall on snowfields, their dark bodies are easy to see. They are also easy to catch when their movements slow in the frozen stillness of the snow crystals.

To the bluebirds, the snow-covered mountain peaks of late summer and early fall must look like crisp, linen tablecloths set for holiday meals. The flocks will leave this alpine setting, however, long before new snow begins to fall and covers all traces of this feast for another year.

Usually by October and at about the same time as the peak of insect abundance, they begin their fall migration.

Even when the weather holds, extending summer into the season of bugling elk, red-leafed willows, and web-spinning spiders, bluebirds disappear from the mountains. Walk through alpine meadows or high ridges where they flew just the week before. All is quiet. Streambanks may be splashed with brilliant fall color, and a late hatch of stoneflies may stir trout to action, but the sky is empty on the high peaks as well as in the nesting valleys. Empty, but peaceful.

It is as if the mountain air has tired of so much activity.

Coyotes, blue grouse, marmots, and many other mountain animals will remain here as the cold months of winter approach. But, as coyotes trot through golden meadows, catching their noses in tangles of spider webs, mountain bluebirds descend to lower elevations. Like geese and swallows, they gather in larger flocks now, some in undulating waves of more than one hundred birds.

Migration begins.

Ron Hirschi

Waxwings flock together, staying in the mountains during times when bluebirds have moved to lower elevations. Like bluebirds, they feed on juniper berries in fall and winter months.

31

Eastern bluebirds also winter in Texas. This male was photographed along the Rio Frio in February.

WINTER

Where will you find bluebirds in winter?

Texas.

Deep in the heart of Texas.

When their summer meadows are winter white and Rocky Mountain coyotes leap through drifting snow to search for tunneling mice, many bluebirds fly south into Texas.

If you do not know Texas well, you might think it is always warm since it is a southern state. It can be warm. It can also be cold; those who live in Texas will tell you of winter snows and strong winds that blow across the Panhandle where mountain bluebirds first arrive in late September or early October.

Those who know the bluebirds of Texas well will tell you that weather seems to have little to do with bluebird abundance in the state from one winter to the next. Some years, the flocks are widespread despite cold weather, apparently because the birds can find plenty to eat. Maybe they have already seen worse in their spring and summer mountains.

Their winter diet includes insects, but they also eat mistletoe, currants, grapes, elderberries, sumac, and other berries. When the fruit of hackberry and juniper is plentiful, bluebirds are especially abundant. In times of poor berry crops, they vanish.

Like so many wintering birds, many bluebirds do not live through this difficult season.

Weather does influence bluebird movements in winter as seen when they move out into open country on mild mornings. Here, bluebirds might feed on beetles, ants, or other insects just as they did in the mountains. The flat, winter landscape may be different from their high meadows. Their feeding techniques are not: Foraging birds stalk their prey from the ground, hover, or watch for fluttering wings from a low perch.

As in other seasons, rivers remain an important part of their lives. When winds whip across the mesquite flats above the river canyons, wintering bluebirds retreat to the shelter of stream bottoms. Most years, they can be seen in large numbers as they are drawn to the banks of the Prairie Dog Fork of the Red, the Palo Duro, and the Canadian rivers.

In summer, bluebirds seem to drink and bathe infrequently in streams. Needed moisture is probably contained in their diet at that time. Dew-drenched plants also offer morning water droplets, tiny diamonds that gather in the cups of lupine leaves.

The dry winter air is a dramatic change. As in summer, the birds are still attracted to rivers for many of the same reasons. Now they flock to the canyons for escape from winds and other weather extremes, to be near drinking and bathing water, and to be near berry crops tucked along the canyon walls.

In Big Spring, Texas, one of the best places to watch wintering bluebirds is at a place that first seems out of character for a bird of the mountain wilderness. For the bluebirds that gather near the golfers at the Country Club, the open grasslands and scattered juniper trees must appear like their natural home. For the golfers and local residents, the bluebirds appear like spring blossoms, adding a welcome splash of color to a West Texas winter.

Texas is an important wintering ground. It is also critical for many other birds. Near Kerrville, for example, more than fifty thousand migratory robins have been seen in some winters. Bluebirds gather in other winter destinations and in some years flocks may move mostly east or west of their nesting mountains rather than fly south.

Eastern extremes within the United States lead them into the middle of Kansas and Oklahoma. To the west, wintering bluebirds have been known to fly out across the open Pacific to islands such as Santa Rosa, off the coast of southern California.

Mountain bluebirds also fly south into the mountains of Mexico, mainly within the northern states. Known southern limits are Michoacán. They have been observed as far east as Nuevo León, not quite to the Gulf of Mexico. Along the West Coast, they can be seen in Baja California.

Farther north, some bluebirds remain quite near their summer mountains. They live in New Mexico and Arizona year-round. Some years, they will stay through winter as far north as the sage deserts of eastern Oregon.

Very little is known about the winter movements on any large scale. What is known comes mainly from a few bird-banding records. One mountain bluebird marked with a band on its leg in 1971 near Edmonton, Alberta, was observed in the fall of 1972 not far north of Amarillo, Texas.

Approximately 1,400 miles separate the two points between the banded bird's birthplace and West Texas. If you could ascend to a great height on warm air currents rising above Amarillo, your view to Alberta would be of a rugged mountainscape

Ron Hirschi

Mountain bluebirds migrate across the high plains of eastern Wyoming, stopping to feed in junipers and sage that grow in this vast expanse.

bordered by the Great Plains. At the heart of that view are the Rocky Mountains where the majority of mountain bluebirds will nest when spring returns.

For some bluebird flocks, the entire plains edge of those mountains is like a highway used during northern and southern migration. For others, the rivers flowing out of the deep contours etched into the mountains are the routes followed each spring and fall. One of the most beautiful landscapes on earth, this mountainous region is changing rapidly along these river valleys and high plains borders.

In years past, many more places along these gentle edges of the mountains supported year-round populations of bluebirds. More land was also available for feeding and resting places needed by migratory and wintering birds.

Now, cities and intensive agriculture spread up and down the river valleys, disrupting animal movements as surely as dams block the free flow of streams. We must use caution and care in developing remaining valleys, foothills, and the high plains. We must also move quickly to protect rivers since streambanks now provide some of the most valuable land for bluebirds and other wildlife.

Sadly, great scars have been torn across much of the West. Bluebirds once flew through winter's end above plains populated by several million prairie chickens. Dust from their spectacular dances now forms tiny shadows cast on ever-diminishing patches of natural prairie. The thunder of endless herds of bison, pronghorn, and wild horses echoed in valleys carved by western rivers. Many of these great streams, born in the same high country as mountain bluebirds, have been silenced like those once numerous animals. The Arkansas River is one example.

Flowing from the Colorado Rockies, the upper Arkansas rushes through spectacular canyons before flowing out into the plains. Here, it becomes a mighty river. Here, too, its life-giving waters are pumped completely dry for agriculture. Corn now grows in the neglected riverbed as it traces a dusty path across Kansas. Birds find little shelter here.

But hope for bluebirds and for other streams remains. That hope comes in part through the actions of people who saw the shelter, the food, and the future of bluebirds and other wildlife threatened in too many ways.

Today bluebirds migrate across the high plains where prairie dogs can still be seen watching the skies for predators. Once, these same open places were home to millions of bison, prairie chickens, and prairie dogs.

Ron Hirschi

A male eastern bluebird at nest box

When my grandfather was young, he lived on a farm. Like many of its time, the farm was small. But it provided most of the family's needs. It also provided most of the needs of deer, wild turkeys, and other wildlife living on the surrounding land. These larger birds and mammals were regarded in much the same way as cattle, chickens, and other domestic animals raised for food.

Hunting was a necessity then, and people followed the whereabouts of game animals very closely. So, we can be more certain of the changes in populations of those larger species than we

ALONG THE BLUEBIRD TRAIL

can of most nonhunted wildlife. Smaller animals, bluebirds included, were observed, but not attended to in as great a detail. Working from sunrise to sunset left little time to watch birds for pleasure.

Grandpa is gone now, so I can't ask him if he remembers bluebirds nesting on his boyhood farm in Iowa. It is likely they did, eastern bluebirds though. These chimney-red-breasted relatives of mountain bluebirds were, like many animals, more common in his youth than today.

Imagine those times: On an evening walk along the fence circling Grandad's farm, you would have seen the last flocks of passenger pigeons flying overhead while fireflies flickered in the pasture grass and whippoorwills called their names from the mulberry trees. Deer would flip their bushy white tails as they leaped past rabbits munching clumps of clover growing around the corn and cucumber plants.

If you leaned against one of the wooden fenceposts that separated the farm from the surrounding woodlands, you might have heard the soft chirp of baby bluebirds. Then, as now, bluebirds nested in woodpecker holes chiseled into the wooden

A male mountain bluebird on a fencepost along a mountain road. Where fences are available mountain bluebirds spend a great deal of time sitting on them, sunning or watching for insects.

fenceposts that were once so much more common throughout America.

If you traveled farther west in those days, you might have ridden your favorite horse across the plains. Riding high in the saddle, you could have seen forever, along miles of fenceline bordering neighboring ranches. Mountain bluebirds would sit atop many of these posts. The wooden fence supports created new nesting places. In fact, bluebird numbers probably increased where the fencelines stretched across the foothills, out onto the plains. On those relatively treeless prairies, the posts created a kind of bluebird trail.

Although they have been pulled up in much of the East, many wooden fenceposts remain in today's West. Even where they have been replaced by metal, the fencelines also remain as a trail of bluebird nesting places. There is one creative differ-ence: People now place birdhouses atop the fenceposts. They do so because of the drastic changes that took place in our country between the late 1800s of my grandfather's youth and today.

The loss of wooden fences in much of the East was one small change that took place as family farms became harder to hold onto. People moved off the land, into cities, and they also began to clear more and more land. More cropland meant fewer weeds that are needed by wildlife. And, former woodlands were also cut to make way for modern, high-tech agriculture.

Ironically, eastern bluebirds disappeared from some areas where thick forests grew up in abandoned farm fields. Unable to feed without cleared pastureland, the bluebirds vanished. Pesti-cides may have been a critical last blow for birds that could still find meadows and natural nesting places. Intense competition for the remaining cavities aggravated the problem.

Regardless of ultimate causes, people noticed an abrupt de-cline in eastern bluebird numbers. A short time later, the same population drops were observed in western bluebirds and for mountain bluebirds living in more settled regions of the western mountains.

Although it seemed impossible to alter the path of land

development eliminating bluebird habitat, people did help bluebirds, one family at a time. They responded by putting up bluebird houses in their yards. Here, birds found safe nesting places with plenty of grass for feeding flights.

Soon, eastern bluebird houses were being put up in playfields, parks, and other open lands. Inspired and supported by groups such as the North American Bluebird Society, people also began to put up nesting boxes for western and mountain bluebirds. Due to an increasing number of nesting places, the birds have returned to former breeding areas.

As eagerly as ranchers stringing a fenceline, many people now design trails of carefully spaced bluebird houses. These trails criss-cross America, extending many miles and uniting people in a common goal that benefits other cavity nesters as well as bluebirds. In Montana alone, more than thirty thousand birds have fledged from boxes put up by a devoted group known as Mountain Bluebird Trails. Farther west, the residents of Bickleton, Washington, proudly proclaim their area to be the "Bluebird Capitol of the World," because of the success of their bluebird trails.

To the south, people in wintering grounds are putting up boxes with insulated walls so that birds can have warm places to roost on cold nights. This may seem an extreme and even silly gesture at first. But many studies have shown that winter survival may be far more important to the future of migratory birds than was previously thought.

Throughout the mountains and high plains, many other needs exist along the invisible trail that mountain bluebirds follow. Some of those needs are becoming better understood. Many are being met by people who build bluebird trails.

These trails built by human carpenters help bluebirds survive into the near future. Hopefully, river valleys, mountain woodlands, alpine meadows, and winter canyons of West Texas will also be protected. Then, we will be assured that bluebirds will always be able to find stoneflies and spiders, juniper and hackberry, and natural homes built by woodpecker architects.

On the bluebird trail

Male mountain bluebird near his nest

I remember well the first mountain bluebird I'd ever seen—a lone male eating tiny insects on a snowfield, high in the Canadian Rockies. It was September and most of the previous year's snow had melted. But, at that elevation, glaciers hold onto accumulations of snowfall through the years. The bluebird's patch of winter white would remain long after the bird flew south.

Since that day, I have watched bluebirds in many other places, often thinking about that first bird. Vivid blue on white, it is a wonderful image to hold onto. His seemingly unusual

41

presence at that elevation was also an interesting puzzle to solve. Why would a bluebird fly up to such heights when much of the year snow is such a threat?

The answer came years later. I watched late summer birds more closely, read about mountain ecology, and I talked with insect experts at the University of Washington. It seems clear that the birds follow spiders to the summits. But, maybe they also come to cool their feet on the warm days of a lingering summer?

Many more questions about bluebirds remain. What do they need most at night? How often do young birds remain with their parents after the nesting season? How many woodpeckers are needed to keep a woodland supplied with adequate bluebird homes? Why are bluebirds so beautiful?

But there are many other beautiful birds. Most aren't even as well understood or protected as bluebirds. As a wildlife biologist, it is my job to watch, photograph, and write about them in attempts to make sure they will not become mere shadows from the past. I only wish there was time to show them all to you, personally.

Even if I just wrote about each of the blue birds, there are so many. Where to begin? With blue buntings in Mexico, Hooded Mountain tanagers in Southern Peru, or blue rock thrushes that live at 16,000 feet in the Himalayas? Or, should I follow the azure-shouldered tanagers of Southeast Brazil, the blue-necked tanagers of the Andes, the blue honeycreepers of Central America, the blue whistling thrushes of Southeast Asia, the magnificent beryl-spangled tanagers of Bolivia, or the blue-fronted lorikeets that are thought to exist on the island of Buru in Indonesia?

Maybe it is best to look more closely in my own backyard where Steller's jays brighten the Pacific Northwest winters. Or, perhaps in the mountain bluebirds' backyards where lazuli buntings perch like tiny blossoms in spring aspens. What wonderful choices. What wonderful reasons to search for them all and try to understand their needs before it is too late.

Steller's jays are among the blue birds that often live very near people.

Ron Hirschi

Even small groves of aspen provide homes for nesting birds.

- Learn more about bluebirds living in your area. If you live on the Pacific side of the Rockies, chances are good that western bluebirds live nearby. All mountains and high plains of the West from Mexico to Alaska offer potential homes for mountain bluebirds. Eastern bluebirds live only on the Atlantic side of the mountains. Search for possible nesting places, then plan actions that will encourage birds to nest.

- If nesting places are not used by bluebirds, build a birdhouse. Write the North American Bluebird Society, P.O. Box 6295, Silver Spring, Maryland 20906-0295. They will send you, at no

APPENDIX: What Can You Do to Help Bluebirds?

charge, plans for a bluebird house along with information about their efforts, including how you might become part of a bluebird trail.

- Learn more about the plants and animals living with bluebirds, especially those that bluebirds need in their neighborhood. Watch for woodpeckers along woodland edges. Search open fields that have wooden fencelines or small groves of trees near meadows. Look for bluebirds in these places each spring. Then, read more about the special needs of each of the plants and animals you observe in these places, discovering what they need to ensure they will return next year. To help identify plants and animals, use a field guide or ask for help from an experienced naturalist. Your local librarian will know the name of a person from the Audubon Society who might be willing to help you get started.

- Plant an aspen tree. Planting a single tree at the edge of an open field may help bluebirds more than any other thing you can do. Someday, your lone aspen may even become a forest since new trees sprout from spreading roots. Then, your aspen grove might become home for woodpeckers, chickadees, and maybe, a nesting pair of bluebirds that will return each spring for years to come.

- Even if you live nowhere near a place that seems right for planting trees or putting up nesting boxes, you might have an idea no one has considered, some valuable idea that might help bluebirds. If so, write your idea, draw a picture of your thoughts, or take a photograph of your creative plan. Then, send it to OUR WILDLIFE, P.O. Box 1137, Suquamish, Washington 98392. They will make sure someone who can help bluebirds will consider your thoughts very carefully.

GLOSSARY

Alpine   Area on a mountain above timberline. Altitude of alpine zone varies with location, generally descending farther north.

Aquatic   Frequents water.

Bird Banding   Activity regulated by the U.S. Fish and Wildlife Service in which numbered (sometimes colored too) metal bands are placed on bird legs to aid in future identification.

Brood (Period)   Time newly hatched birds are kept warm by the parent. Mother bluebirds cover their young, keeping their sparsely feathered bodies warm with her own body and feathers.

Competition   There are degrees of competition, but two animals are not usually said to compete until the *same* resource is sought by both: Bluebirds and tree swallows compete since they both need the same size nest cavity and entry hole. Bluebirds and buffleheads do not compete even though both are cavity nesters; buffleheads require a larger entry hole.

Dipper   Also known as water ouzels, these aquatic birds live along streams from Alaska to Central America.

Fledgling   Young bird that has just left the nest. Time of fledging varies greatly among birds and those with a long nestling period often have greater survival difficulties.

Glaciated   Glaciers form when snowfall is greater than snowmelt; areas covered by glaciers are said to be glaciated. The Columbia Icefields between Jasper and Banff National Parks in Canada offer close views of spectacularly glaciated mountains.

Gossamer   This word is rich in its full meaning. Derived from a time of year once known as Goosesummer, it now refers to the silky threads of spider webs that appear in that season just before fall.

High Plains   Region just to the east of the Rocky Mountains. The plains rise from the farms and remnant prairies of the Midwest, providing significant habitat for prairie wildlife and wintering animals of the mountains.

Incubation   Time young birds develop within the egg while parents (in bluebirds, only females) sit on the nest to keep the eggs warm.

45

Insecticide Poisons intended to kill insects that often kill birds, fish, and other animals too.

Interrelationships Complex connections between plants, animals, and their surroundings.

Latitude Distance from the equator, measured in degrees both north and south.

Metamorphosis Change of form, as when a stonefly undergoes metamorphosis from an aquatic nymph to a flying adult.

Monogamous Having only one mate during a lifetime.

Nestling Baby bird during time spent within the nest after hatching.

Nymph A preadult form many insects go through. The nymph typically lives in water and lacks wings.

Pesticides Poisons that kill a variety of plants and animals. Once thought capable of destroying only undesirable species, pesticides and their residues kill or adversely affect others in complex ways, often by increasing their concentration as they pass through food webs.

Riffle Stream segment where broken water bubbles over stones.

Sedge Grasslike plant with sharp edges.

Snag Old, dying, or dead trees that often turn silver-gray in the weather and usually offer a valuable home for cavity-nesting birds and mammals.

Territorial Boundaries Invisible lines surrounding a defended place of importance such as the bluebird's nest, nearby meadow, and resting perches.

Territory Defended area.

Wilderness Area Wilderness usually refers to the wild countryside. But the Cloud Peak Wilderness Area and other lands with this designation are legally protected under the Wilderness Act of 1964. To protect special places, most damaging activities are prohibited and travel is off limits for motor vehicles.

Zugunruhe Premigratory restlessness, including a decrease in hours spent sleeping.